I LOVE YOU SKY HIGH

JACKIE MACGIRVIN
ILLUSTRATED BY PAT JESSEE

Little Bear giggled as Mama Bear
gently tucked the blanket under
his fuzzy chin.

"Do you love me?" he asked.

"You know I love you" replied Mama
Bear with a big smile. "I love you as high
as the sky and as many as the stars."

"Mama, tell me the story again."

~ 4 ~

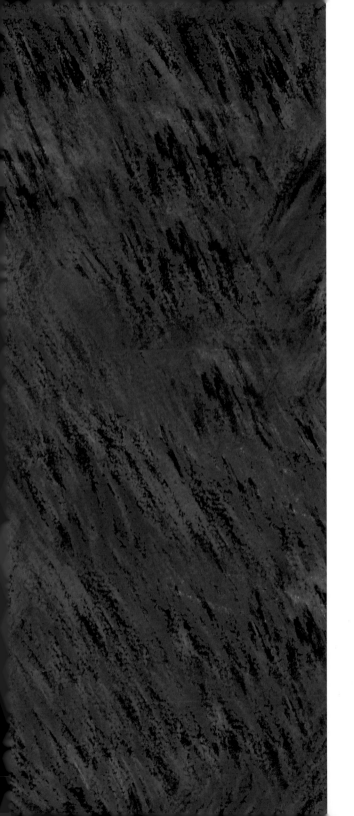

"On the day you were born, my love for you grew so big that it swirled around the earth setting the winds in motion."

"It swooshed above the red-roofed barns and green pastures where Cow and her calf grazed."

The artist has hidden a picture of a monkey somewhere in this picture. Can you find it?

"Can you find it high above the river?"
(Look behind the trees.)

Where is the hidden picture of a cat's face? Meow, meow!

"It stirred up dust in hidden copper-colored canyons."

"It zipped over kite-flying puppies
on a sandy beach."

Can you find the hidden picture of the dog's head?

"Then my love for you streaked across the night sky, lighting the grassy field below."

"It bounced on the ocean waves and lifted
flying seagulls high in the sky."

"My love for you soared over the
tippy-top of the whole wide world,
the cold, snowy North Pole."
(Hello, mommy and baby Polar Bears.)

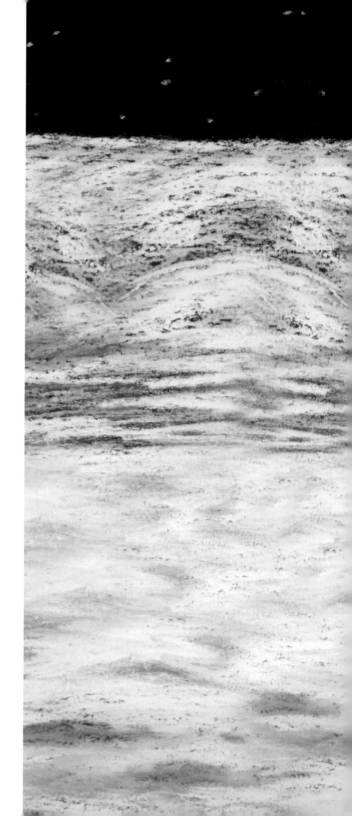

Do you see an alligator hiding in the snow?
Brrrrrrr! He doesn't think you'll find him!

"It flew higher, sending the clouds swirling through the sky and bright lightning crackling back to earth."

Do you see the hidden peacock?

"It grew so big nothing could hold it back.
My love for you flew right up
into outer space."

Can you find the hidden frog?
What sound does he make?

"It banged right into the moon leaving large craters then it bounced toward the sun."

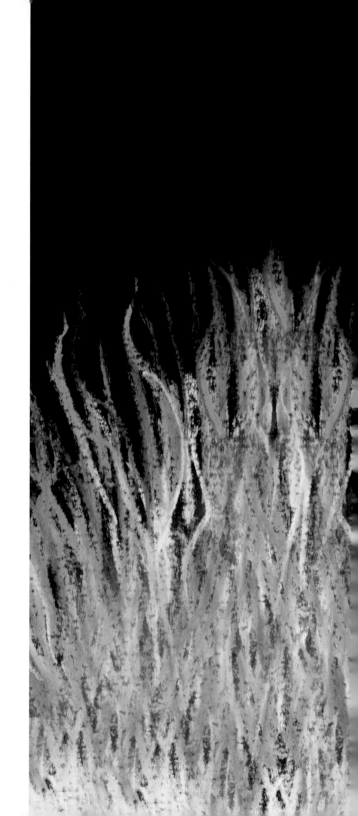

"There was a white-hot flash,
then a big explosion
flung little pieces of light far across
the silent darkness."

Mama Bear opened the curtain.
"Always remember when you gaze into
the night sky,
each star is a picture of my love for you,
because I love you sky high and as many
as the stars."

"Mama," he said, "Tell it again."

ANSWER KEY FOR THE HIDDEN PICTURES

Page 9 - Monkey

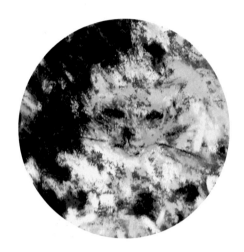

Page 11 - Cat

Page 15 - Dog

Page 21 - Alligator

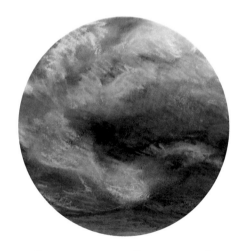

Page 23 - Peacock

Page 25 - Frog

Can you name the animals in this book? Which animal is your favorite?
Can you name the letters on this page?

MY DRAWINGS

Draw the animal from this book you would like as a pet.

Draw the sun in the sky.

Can you write the book's title here?
How many pages does it have?

Draw the doggie's kite.

By _____ Age_____

Draw baby bear's face here.

Pick a planet to draw from page 25.

Do you love your mother as high as the sky and as many as the stars? Draw the stars here.

What would you like to draw?

DEDICATION

Jackie Macgirvin: This book is dedicated to my own Little Bear, Calvin and his three cubs, Wesley, Benji and Lucy. I wrote this book when Calvin was young and he is now in his early 30's so I guess it's time. I am also grateful to my awesome friend Pat for doing the fabulous illustrations and prodding me along the path to publication. Without her this text would still be hibernating on my hard drive.

Pat Jessee: I dedicate this book to my wonderful husband, Lance, who helped me so much with the technical side of things and to my three adult children and four grandchildren to let them all know that
I Love You Sky High!

ABOUT THE AUTHOR AND ILLUSTRATOR

Jackie Macgirvin is an award-winning author, editor and screenwriter. In addition to writing all kinds of books she helps frustrated writers polish their stories and get them published. ChristianBookDoctor.com JackieMacgirvin5@gmail.com

Pat Jessee: My dad was an artist and told me "I put a pencil in your hand when you were two and you've been drawing ever since." A few years ago I met Jackie in a small group and we became friends. She saw the animal paintings I did for my granddaughter's bedroom and a new relationship was born as we collaborated on this children's picture book. Visit patjesseecreations.com to view more of my art.

The inspiration for this book was Psalm 36:5

"Your lovingkindness, O LORD, extends to the heavens,

Your faithfulness reaches to the skies" (NASB).